THE BREAKING NEWS

WRITTEN & ILLUSTRATED BY SARAH LYNNE REUL

ROARING BROOK
New York

I remember when we heard
the bad news.

Suddenly Mom is glued to the television.

Dad can't stop checking his phone.

They whisper
and I pretend not to hear.

It is more than a little scary.

Mom forgets
to tuck me in.

Dad is too tired for
bedtime stories.

At school, my teacher says
to look for the helpers.

Even when the news is bad, you can still find good people trying to make things better in big and small ways.

I want to help in a **BIG** way.

I decide to put on the funniest show
ever to make everyone laugh again . . .

but the grown-ups
don't feel like
laughing.

GRANDMA'S HOUSE

SCHOOL

DAD

MOM

OLLIE

ME

BELLA

I tell them about
the force fields I'll invent
to keep us all safe . . .
but their smiles are
tiny and sad.

I try to be on my BEST behavior all the time, to be so, so good . . . but they hardly even notice.

I think maybe there is nothing I can do to help in a big way.

I feel small.

So maybe . . .

I can try to do . . .

just one . . .

small thing?

And maybe another . . .

and another . . .

and one more?

Small things don't solve everything.

The bad news is still there, after all.

But
then
again . . .

SO . . .

are . . .

we.

For my mom, Janet Cohen, who gave me words
and taught me how to help plants grow,

and for my dad, Bob Reul, who gave me pictures
and showed me how to read, and read, and read.